The River Bank

from
The Wind in the Willows

Written by
KENNETH GRAHAME

Abridged and illustrated by
INGA MOORE

TED SMART

The River Bank

The Mole had been working hard all the morning, spring-cleaning his little home. First with brooms, then with dusters; then on ladders and steps and chairs, with a brush and a pail of whitewash; till he had dust in his throat and eyes, and splashes of whitewash all over his black fur, and an aching back and weary arms. Spring was moving in the air above and in the earth below, around even his dark and lowly little house, and suddenly he flung down his brush, said "Bother!" and "O blow!" and also "Hang spring-cleaning!" and bolted out of the house without even waiting to put on his coat. Making for the steep tunnel which answered in his case to the gravelled drive owned by animals whose residences are nearer to the sun and air, he scraped and scratched and scrabbled and scrooged, then he scrooged again and scrabbled and scraped, muttering, "Up we go! Up we go!" till at last ...

pop! his snout came out into the sunlight, and he found himself rolling in the warm grass of a great meadow.

"This is fine," he said to himself. "This is better than whitewashing!"

Jumping off all his four legs at once, in the joy of living and spring without its cleaning, he pursued his way across the meadow till he reached the further side.

He rambled busily along the hedgerows, across copses, finding everywhere birds building, flowers budding, leaves thrusting.

As he meandered aimlessly along, suddenly he stood by the edge of a full-fed river. Never in his life had he seen a river before. All was a-shake and a-shiver – gleams and sparkles, chatter and bubble. The Mole was bewitched. By its side he trotted spellbound; and when tired at last, he sat on the bank.

As he sat and looked across to the bank opposite, a dark hole just above the water's edge caught his eye and dreamily he fell to considering what a snug dwelling-place it would make for an animal with few wants and fond of a bijou riverside residence, when something bright and small seemed to twinkle down in the heart of it like a tiny star. But it could hardly be a star. Then, as he looked, it winked at him, and so declared itself to be an eye; and a small face began gradually to grow up round it, like a frame round a picture.

A brown face with whiskers.

A grave round face, with a twinkle in its eye.

Small neat ears and thick silky hair.

It was the Water Rat!

"Hullo, Mole!" said the Water Rat.

"Hullo, Rat!" said the Mole.

"Would you like to come over?" inquired the Rat presently.

"O, it's all very well to *talk*!" said the Mole rather pettishly, he being new to a river and riverside life and its ways.

The Rat said nothing, but stooped and unfastened a rope and hauled on it; then lightly stepped into a little boat. It was painted blue outside and white within and was just the size for two animals; and the Mole's whole heart went out to it at once.

The Rat sculled smartly across and made fast. Then he held up his fore-paw as the Mole stepped gingerly down and, to his surprise, found himself actually seated in the stern of a real boat.

"This has been a wonderful day!" said he, as the Rat shoved off and took the sculls again. "Do you know, I've never been in a boat before in all my life."

"What?" cried the Rat, open-mouthed. "Never been in a – you never – well, I – what have you been doing, then?"

"Is it so nice as all that?" asked the Mole shyly.

"Nice? It's the *only* thing," said the Water Rat solemnly, as he leant forward for his stroke. "Believe me, my friend, there is *nothing* – absolutely nothing – half so much worth doing as simply messing about in boats. Simply messing," he went on dreamily: "messing – about – in – boats; messing – "

"Look ahead, Rat!" cried Mole suddenly.

It was too late. The boat struck the bank full tilt. The Rat lay on his back at the bottom of the boat, his heels in the air.

" – about in boats," he went on, picking himself up with a pleasant laugh. "Look here! If you've really nothing else on this morning, supposing we drop down the river together and have a long day of it?"

The Mole waggled his toes from sheer happiness, spread his chest with a sigh and leaned back blissfully into the soft cushions. "*What* a day I'm having!" he said. "Let us start at once!"

"Hold hard a minute, then!" said the Rat. He looped the painter through a ring in his landing-stage, climbed up into his hole above and reappeared staggering under a fat wicker luncheon-basket.

"Shove that under your feet," he observed to the Mole. Then he untied the painter and took the sculls again.

"What's inside it?" asked the Mole, wriggling with curiosity.

"There's cold chicken inside it," replied the Rat briefly;

"coldtonguecoldhamcoldbeefpickledgherkinssaladfrenchrolls cresssandwichespottedmeatgingerbeerlemonadesodawater—"

"O stop, stop," cried the Mole in ecstasies: "This is too much!"

"Do you really think so?" inquired the Rat seriously. "It's only what I always take and the other animals tell me I'm a mean beast and cut it *very* fine!"

The Mole never heard a word he was saying. Absorbed in the new life, the scents and the sounds and the sunlight, he trailed a paw in the water and dreamed waking dreams. The Water Rat, like the good fellow he was, sculled on.

"I like your clothes awfully, old chap," he remarked after some half hour or so. "I'm going to get a black velvet smoking-suit myself some day."

"I beg your pardon," said the Mole, pulling himself together with an effort. "You must think me very rude; but all this is so new to me. So – this – is – a – River!"

"*The* River," corrected the Rat.

"And you really live by it? What a jolly life!"

"By it and with it and on it and in it," said the Rat. "It's my world, and I don't want any other."

"But isn't it a bit dull at times?" the Mole ventured to ask. "Just you and the river, and no one else to pass a word with?"

"No one else to — well, of course," said the Rat. "You're new to it. The bank is so crowded nowadays that many people are moving away altogether. O no, it isn't what it used to be, at all. Kingfishers, dabchicks, moorhens about all day long always wanting you to *do* something."

"What lies over *there*?" asked the Mole, waving a paw towards a wood that darkly framed the water-meadows on one side.

"That? O, that's just the Wild Wood," said the Rat shortly. "We don't go there very much, we river-bankers."

"Aren't they — aren't they very *nice* people there?" said the Mole a trifle nervously.

"W-e-ll," replied the Rat, "the squirrels are all right. *And* the rabbits — some of 'em, but rabbits are a mixed lot. And then there's Badger. He lives right in the heart of it. Dear old Badger! Nobody interferes with *him*!"

"Why, who *should* interfere with him?" asked the Mole.

"Well, of course — there — are others," explained the Rat. "Weasels — and stoats — foxes — and so on. They're all right in a way, but they break out sometimes, there's no denying it and — you can't really trust them, that's the fact!"

"And beyond the Wild Wood?" asked the Mole.

"The Wide World," said the Rat. "And that doesn't matter."

Leaving the main stream, they passed into what seemed like a land-locked lake. Green turf sloped down to either edge, while ahead of them the silvery shoulder of a weir, arm-in-arm with a mill-wheel, that held up in its turn a grey-gabled mill-house, filled the air with a soothing murmur of sound.

It was so very beautiful that the Mole could only hold up both paws

and gasp, "O my! O my! O my!"

The Rat brought the boat alongside the bank, made her fast, helped the Mole ashore and swung out the luncheon-basket. The Mole begged to be allowed to unpack it all by himself. The Rat was very pleased to indulge him and to sprawl on the grass and rest while his excited friend shook out the tablecloth and spread it, took out the mysterious packets one by one and arranged their contents in due order, still gasping "O my! O my!" When all was ready, the Rat said, "Pitch in, old fellow!" and the Mole was very glad to obey, for he had started his spring-cleaning very early that morning, and had not paused for a bite since.

"What are you looking at?" asked the Rat presently, when the Mole's eyes were able to wander off the tablecloth a little.

"I am looking," said the Mole, "at a streak of bubbles travelling along the surface of the water."

"Bubbles? Oho!" said the Rat.

A broad, glistening muzzle showed itself above the bank, and the Otter hauled himself out and shook the water from his coat.

"Greedy beggars!" he observed. "Why didn't you invite me, Ratty?"

"Such a rumpus everywhere!" he continued. "All the world seems out on the river today. I came up this backwater to get a moment's peace — and stumble on you fellows! At least — I beg your pardon — I don't exactly mean that."

There was a rustle behind them from a hedge, where last year's leaves still clung thick and a stripy head peered forth.

"Come on, old Badger!" shouted the Rat.

The Badger trotted forward a pace or two; then grunted "H'm! Company," turned his back and disappeared.

"That's *just* the sort of fellow he is!" observed the disappointed Rat. "Simply hates Society! We shan't see any more of him today. Well, tell us, *who's* out on the river?"

"Toad's out, for one," replied the Otter. "In his brand-new wager-boat; new togs, new everything!"

The two animals looked at each other and laughed.

"Once, it was nothing but sailing," said the Rat. "Then he tired of that and took to punting. Last year it was house-boating, and we all had to go with him and pretend we liked it. It's all the same, whatever he takes up; he gets tired of it, and starts on something fresh."

"Such a good fellow, too," remarked the Otter. "But no stability – especially in a boat!"

From where they sat they could get a glimpse of the main stream across the island that separated them; and just then a wager-boat flashed into view, the rower – a short stout figure – splashing badly and rolling a good deal, but working his hardest. The Rat stood up and hailed him, but Toad – for it was he – shook his head and settled sternly to his work.

"He'll be out of the boat in a minute," said the Rat, sitting down again.

"Of course he will," chuckled the Otter. "Did I ever tell you that story…"

A Mayfly swerved athwart the current.
A swirl of water and a "cloop!" and
the Mayfly was visible no more.

Neither was the Otter.

Again there was a streak of
bubbles on the surface of the river.

"Well," the Rat said. "I suppose we ought to be moving on.
I wonder which of us had better pack the luncheon-basket?"

"O, let me," said the Mole. So, of course, the Rat let him.

Packing the basket was not quite such pleasant work as
unpacking the basket. It never is. But the Mole was bent on
enjoying everything, and although just when he had got the job
done he saw a plate staring up at him from the grass, and then a
fork which anybody ought to have seen, and last of all the
mustard-pot – still, somehow, the thing got finished at last,
without much loss of temper.

The afternoon sun was getting low as the Rat sculled gently homewards, murmuring poetry things, and not paying much attention to Mole. But the Mole was full of lunch, and self-satisfaction, and pride, and already quite at home in a boat (so he thought) and presently he said, "Ratty! Please, *I* want to row!"

The Rat shook his head with a smile. "Not yet," he said. "Wait till you've had a few lessons. It's not so easy as it looks."

The Mole began to feel more and more jealous of Rat, sculling so strongly and easily along. His pride began to whisper he could do it every bit as well, and after a minute or two he suddenly jumped up and seized the sculls. The Rat, who was gazing out over the water, was taken by surprise. He fell backwards off his seat with his legs in the air for the second time, while the triumphant Mole took his place.

"Stop it, you *silly* ass!" cried the Rat from the bottom of the boat. "You'll have us over!"

The Mole flung his sculls back with a flourish and made a great dig at the water. He missed the surface altogether, his legs flew up above his head, and he found himself lying on top of the Rat. He made a grab at the side of the boat and the next moment – Sploosh!

Over went the boat, and he found himself struggling in the water.

O my, how cold the water was, and O, how *very* wet it felt. How it sang in his ears as he went down, down, down! How bright and welcome the sun looked as he rose to the surface. How black was his despair when he found himself sinking again! Then a firm paw gripped him by the back of his neck. It was the Rat, and he was laughing – the Mole could *feel* him laughing, right down his arm and through his paw.

The Rat got hold of a scull and shoved it under the Mole's arm, then he did the same by the other side of him and, swimming behind, propelled him to shore.

The Mole sat on the bank, a squashy lump of misery. When the Rat had rubbed him down a bit, and wrung some of the wet out of him, he said, "Now then, old fellow! Trot up and down the towing-path till you're dry, while I dive for the luncheon-basket."

So the dismal Mole, wet without and ashamed within, trotted about while the Rat plunged into the water again, righted the boat, fetched his floating property and finally dived for the luncheon-basket.

When all was ready the Mole, limp and dejected, took his seat in the stern of the boat. "Ratty!" he said as they set off, in a voice broken with emotion, "I am very sorry. I've been a complete ass, and I know it. To think I might have lost that beautiful luncheon-basket. Will you overlook it this once and let things go on as before?"

"That's all right," said Rat cheerily. "What's a little wet to a Water Rat? I'm more in the water than out of it most days. Don't you think any more about it; look here! I think you had better come and stop with me for a time. I'll teach you to row and swim and you'll soon be as handy on the water as any of us."

The Mole was so touched by his kind manner he could find no voice to answer him; and he had to brush away a tear or two with the back of his paw. But the Rat kindly looked in another direction and soon the Mole's spirits revived and he was even able to give some back-talk to a couple of moorhens who were sniggering to each other about his bedraggled appearance.

When they got home, the Rat made a bright fire in the parlour, and planted the Mole in an arm-chair, in front of it, in dressing gown and slippers, and told him river stories until supper-time. Very thrilling stories they were, too, to an earth-dwelling animal like Mole. Stories about weirs and sudden floods, leaping pike, and herons, adventures down drains and night-fishings with Otter, or excursions far afield with Badger.

Supper was a cheerful meal, but shortly afterwards a terribly sleepy Mole had to be escorted upstairs to the best bedroom, where he laid his head on his pillow in great peace and contentment, knowing that his new-found friend, the River, was lapping the sill of his window.